On Forbidden Ground

by
TJ Perkins

PublishAmerica
Baltimore

First printing

ISBN: 1-4137-5001-X
PUBLISHED BY PUBLISHAMERICA, LLLP
www.publishamerica.com
Baltimore

Printed in the United States of America

More Mysteries by TJ Perkins

Fantasies are Murder

The Secret in Phantom Forest

Trade Secret

Image in the Tapestry

Wound Too Tight

Mystery of the Attic

To my dearest friend, Lynn. Thanks for all your love, support, and belief in my writing. Rest in peace, I'll miss you.

Table of Contents

Chapter 1: The Mysterious Letter   9

Chapter 2: Unanswered Questions   14

Chapter 3: The Missing Lawyer   17

Chapter 4: A Piece to the Puzzle   20

Chapter 5: An Unexpected Visitor   23

Chapter 6: The Old House   28

Chapter 7: A Grave Mistake   33

Chapter 8: The Sink Hole   36

Chapter 9: On Forbidden Ground   41

Chapter 10: Trapped   44

Chapter 11: The Confrontation   49

Chapter 12: A Near Miss   54

Chapter 13: An Alternate Route   56

Chapter 14: The Rise of the Crystal   60

Chapter 15: A Worthwhile Demise   65

Chapter 16: An Uncertain Rescue   70

Chapter 17: Fate of the Old House   74

Chapter One
The Mysterious Letter

"Give me something more mysterious…you know…*really* scary. This zombie thing will never scare the kids," my boss Mr. McDermond complained while shaking his head and slapping my drawing with the back of his fingers. "It's gotta be gut grabbing, Melissa—something that will be a *real* attention getter for this Halloween's advertising campaign.

"And you really don't think a walking zombie will scare the kids?" I asked in a flat tone, just to be sure of where he was going with his ranting, and remembering a situation that I got myself into back when I was thirteen; my thoughts on this past experience now interrupted by Mr. McDermond's grumpy, loud voice.

"I don't see how. Besides, this looks too nice, too much like he's smiling and coming over for dinner." He paused and looked at my work once more, this time at arms length, squinting his eyes and turning it first from one side and then to the other. After a moment of silence, he let out a sigh and handed the drawing back to me. "Yeah, too nice…hmmm, make it scary."

"Okay, if that's what you want." I hesitated for a moment and glanced at the drawing I had come up with for Mr. McDermond's advertising campaign for a box of Ghoulie's cereal. It was a picture of a walking zombie, arms loaded with boxes of Ghoulie's cereal. The Zombie is smiling and stuffing his face with handfuls of the stuff, while making his way back to his crypt. I thought it was rather ingenious and did all I could to make the character kid-friendly. "Are you sure I should make him *really* scary?" I asked, taking care not to offend my boss and owner of the company where I worked.

"Sure. Why not? With the way kids are today, how could a walking zombie possibly scare anybody?" He smirked and rocked back in his big leather office chair, as he put a foot up on his cherry wood desk.

I turned away and headed slowly for the door. "You have no idea," I mumbled to myself, scowling. I hated it when he shot down my work. I'd spent weeks coming up with an idea for him, another month designing the cereal box, and within five minutes he kills my idea and sends me back to the drawing board. The life of an artist in the advertising business was tough. All my art teachers told me it wasn't going to be easy, even my old teacher Mrs. Moore said she became an art teacher after being trampled on too many times in the field. I tried to keep all of that in mind as I stormed back to my station. The life of an artist, huh! I try so hard for him and he always finds a way to rub both success and failure in my face at the same time. I don't know how I ever became his lead designer!

"He shot down your idea," Tia said, leaning over the divider of our workspaces. Apparently she heard my heavy footsteps of frustration, and felt she should pay me a visit.

"Once again—go figure!" I opened my eyes wide and released a deep breath, and then flopped the drawing down on my desk. "He said it wasn't scary enough." I imitated my boss by sporting a cocky grin and crossing my eyes, which made Tia giggle.

"You know you're his girl, Melissa. Don't let him get to you." Tia was always a good friend and right now her sincere charm and easy-going attitude was just what I needed to calm me down.

"I know," I finally mumbled, looking down at my desk and organizing pencils, charcoal pieces and paint brushes in a small narrow flowerpot. "He said that a walking zombie wouldn't scare kids of today. He has no idea what scary is."

"And you do?" Tia came around the divider and stood next to my desk, looking at me with her arms crossed as she waited for a response.

I looked into her dark brown eyes then ran my fingers over my drawing again. "W-well, I, um…" I stammered, avoiding my co-worker's hard gaze and mocking grin. "You know, everybody has their own opinion of what scary really is."

"And what's *your* idea?" Tia said as she pressed the issue. For some reason it really bothered me that I was on the verge of telling her about my childhood experience, the very thing that still haunted my dreams at night, and the thing that I would never be able to forget—the walking in the attic and the terrible haunting in the old farmhouse.

"Um, I really don't think I should draw a scary zombie, with flesh hanging off of its bones, tattered clothing, or anything like that. Scary on a gown-up level is one thing, but if you put a gown-up scary thing in front of a kid, it could cause mental issues." I plopped down in my chair, slid the drawing in front of me, and then grabbed a clean piece of drawing paper, all the while avoiding eye contact.

Tia giggled at my comment and put her hands on her hips. "It's a design on a cereal box for Halloween, girl. You don't have to go all out, like, blood squirting or something like that. I'm sure he's not asking you to draw death and mayhem."

"No, but I know what scary really is to a kid and I have no intention on drawing something like that," I said, looking up at her with a serious expression on my face.

Tia's dark complexion took on a pale haze and a look of concern showed in her eyes. She was a good friend and co-worker, but at times a bit nosey, and I just wasn't ready to tell anyone about my experiences until I knew them well enough. The only person I knew I could trust was my stepsister, Becky, and I hardly saw her anymore. And trying to talk to my mom or step-dad about the happenings in the old house we used to live in was like talking to a brick wall, because they never believed me. Now, here I was, twenty-one, the lead artist and designer for McDermond's Design Corp., living on my own and calling my own shots in life and I still can't seem to let go of my upsetting past. It was an experience like none other, and I could still hear the sounds of the walking in the attic echoing in my head.

I broke off from my daydreaming and smiled at Tia, who had been watching me closely the entire time.

"Are you all right?" she said, peering at me as if I were a science experiment.

"Hello ladies!" came a loud and cheerful voice from behind us. Ted, the mail delivery guy from the company in-house postal service, had arrived with his rolling bag of mail, making his rounds to drop off packages and letters to all the employees on each of the four floors of McDermond's Design Corp. Normally Ted would get on my nerves because he only stopped by our cubicles for a chance to speak with Tia. This time however, I was grateful for the interruption because I didn't want to get into a heavy conversation with her about my past.

"Hi Ted," Tia said, smiling so big I thought her perfect, bright white teeth would blind him.

"Hello-o Miss Sweetman, and how are you today?"

"Just fine," Tia giggled and twirled her long braids around her fingers.

"Yes, I can see that…" Ted began, but I quickly cut him off.

"Have any mail for me today, Ted?" I said, tapping his huge bicep with my pencil.

"Yes ma'am, a letter." He handed me an envelope that looked really old and worn out, as if it was dropped in the dirt one too many times. I slowly turned it over and noticed that there was neither a postal stamp nor a return address. Immediately I thought it was from someone selling something and dropped it in the trash without opening.

Once Ted and Tia finished flirting, he moved on down the row of cubicles delivering mail and she went back to work, forgetting I never answered her earlier question. Finally, our work area was quiet once more, so I could concentrate on fixing this drawing. *Scary, he wants it scary,* I thought grimly and ran my pencil over the fresh piece of paper, while trying to formulate a new idea. I was so involved in what I was doing that I almost didn't notice a short gust of wind blow across the back of my head and gently move my shoulder length hair from side to side. Thinking someone was playing a joke, I turned around; no one was behind me, no one had a fan pointing my way, and no windows were open. Strange. I turned my attention back to the new drawing.

"Melissa," came a faint whisper of my name. I turned around again to see if someone was close by—still no one. But I heard it; I knew I did. I let out a sigh, shook my head, and began adding charcoal to my drawing; rubbing it in where I wanted it shaded, and I heard my name again. "Melissa." This time, the creepy whisper sounded as if someone was growling my name and I started feeling very upset over this whole thing. *Where was it coming from?* It definitely sounded close by…right in my workspace. My gaze fell on the envelope I had thrown in the trash, and as I stared at it, the sound of faint whispering floated up from it. Just as I reached out my hand, the whispering stopped, and something in my gut told me that I should open it.

Chapter Two
Unanswered Questions

Even though the envelope had no return address anywhere on the outside, the letter inside was of top quality bond, with the name of Mr. William Anderson, Attorney, as well as his address and phone number, on the letterhead. The letter was short and to the point:

Dear Miss Grey,
It is my duty to inform you that you have inherited 27 Wakefield Road in the town of New Windsor, Maryland. Please call for an appointment so that we may convey this property to you in the appropriate legal fashion.

There was no signature, only the typewritten name of Mr. William Anderson, Attorney. I felt a cold shiver run up my spine at the thought of actually owning the old eighteen-century farmhouse where my mother, stepfather, stepsister, and I lived for two strange and unnerving years where I learned the meaning of scary. The place where I not only befriended the spirit of a boy named Josh and went to great lengths to make his murder known to the public so he could rest in peace, but also made an enemy of a crazed, evil spirit of a boy named William, the one who murdered Josh. If it wasn't for my art teacher, Mrs. Moore, I would've never been able to capture the spirit of William in a pyramid-shaped crystal and bury him forever in the cold, dark ground.

The old house had become a quiet, normal house once the spirits left, but then my mom decided to take a job paying more money in the growing town of Westminster and we had to move—again.

I turned the letter over in my hands and read it several more times. It was strange that I was getting this letter. Why hadn't the house gone to the new owner's son or daughter? I know my mother kept in contact with John and his wife Donna after they had finished renovations and moved in. John would always call with a question about the pipes, the thermostat, or something like that. We also stopped by for a short visit a few times because our mail was still being delivered to the old place and Mom wanted to pick it up personally. Every time we visited, I always asked John's kids, John Jr. and Kathy, if they ever heard any weird sounds, like walking in the attic, but they said no and looked at me as if I was a freak. But that was years ago and I felt things must have changed horribly for the worse.

Now my curiosity was running wild. *What happened to John and Donna? Where were their kids? If all of them were gone or missing, how was it that I inherited that old house?* I needed some answers fast, so I called the lawyer's office that had sent me the mysterious letter.

"Mr. Anderson's office, may I help you?" came a stuffy female voice on the other end of the line.

"Hi, my name is Melissa Grey and I received a letter from your office about 27 Wakefield Road."

"Oh, yes, Miss Grey. Mr. Anderson has been waiting for your call, but he's not in right now. If you would just come by the office as soon as you can, I have all the necessary paperwork for you to pick up, as well as the keys to your house."

"But I have a lot of questions to ask Mr. Anderson. What happened to the previous owners? Why did they leave this house to me? Why…"

"Any time during the week would be fine. We'll see you then," the secretary said, abruptly cutting off my string of questions, and then hung up on me.

I was shocked by the way the conversation ended, and although I had never inherited anything before, this whole situation just didn't feel right, it wasn't being done professionally, and possibly not in a completely legal manner. Determined to get to the bottom of this whole mess, I decided to go to the lawyer's office first thing in the morning and find out exactly what was going on.

Chapter Three
The Missing Lawyer

The office of Attorney William Anderson was located at 324 Main Street in downtown New Windsor. A prosperous little town, New Windsor's old eighteenth century buildings were renovated, updated, and made to look and function like brand new. Most of these old homes on Main Street were turned into offices and occupied space next to tall new buildings. It surprised me to see how past and present blended so well together; the old brick buildings looking very nice next to the dark newer brick buildings, many of which had fresh paint, new windows and flower pots spilling over with beautiful flowers and vines.

Finding parking on Main Street at nine o'clock in the morning was usually a big problem, and I was shocked that I got a spot directly in front of the attorney's office. Putting a quarter in the meter, and ignoring strange looks from a few passersby, I entered the office, anxious to get some of my questions answered. Unfortunately no one was in; the door was open, the air conditioner was running, a cup of steaming coffee from the nearby Starbuck's was sitting on what I presumed was the secretary's desk, but she wasn't in. The office wasn't very big; and being part of what was left of an old eighteen-century house, it only had two big rooms with a desk each, and I guessed one room was for Mr. Anderson, the other for an associate, and the spacious entrance room had a desk for his secretary. There wasn't very much furniture in the office and, since the house was so old, I didn't find it strange that the wood floor sounded exceptionally hollow and squeaked dreadfully in certain places as I paced around searching for someone to talk to.

"Hello? Is anybody here?" I called while opening a few closed doors, and discovered the bathroom and a closet. I then went over to the secretary's desk and noticed a large manila envelope with my name and a sticky note on the front. The note read:

Miss Grey,

Inside you will find all the pertinent paperwork. Please sign in the highlighted spaces, keep the copies marked client copy, and take the key. I'm sorry that I can't be here, but I had an unexpected appointment.

"Only one key? That's odd."

Again, there was no signature, only the initials W.A. at the bottom of the note. Shaking my head at how unprofessional this lawyer was, I opened the envelope and took out the paperwork. I sat down at the secretary's desk and started reading each page, while still trying to ignore the odd looks I kept getting from people as they walked by the office.

"I don't know what their problem is," I mumbled and shook my head.

An hour passed and still no one had come back to the office. *What kind of secretary would open the place, leave her hot cup of coffee, which was now cold, and not return?* I thought to myself. I almost felt guilty that I would have to leave soon and the office door would not be locked, but it's not my problem and I'm not going to worry about it.

I turned my attention back to the papers conveying ownership of the old eighteenth century house into my name, and hesitated to sign. I really didn't want that house, there were too many bad memories, and I still didn't know why the place was being given to me and not John and Donna's kids. Getting fed up with the whole not knowing thing, I shoved the papers back into the envelope, put the key to the house in my pants pocket and walked out of the office. John's son, John Griffin, Jr. lived in town somewhere near the middle school, and I was going to hunt him down and talk with him before I signed anything. Since Mr. William Anderson couldn't be around to explain things to me and get his properly signed copies; I felt it was only fair to do some investigating on my own first, and deliver his signed papers when I got a chance.

I left in a huff, got in my little navy blue Volvo, and sped toward the middle school.

Chapter Four
A Piece to the Puzzle

The elderly residents of the first house I decided to stop at could only guess at which house John Jr. lived in. They felt it was further down the road, about one block, with the while picket fence. I zoomed down to the house, parked near the curb, and ran up to the front door. To my surprise, the door flew open just as I was getting ready to knock. An elderly African-American lady stood in the doorway grinning from ear to ear; her dark eyes dazzled behind the glasses she wore, the lenses as thick as the bottom of a Coke bottle, and her tiny, frail body seemed to tremble nervously.

"Ooooo, I have a visitor," she said, reaching her soft, wrinkled hands towards mine.

As she was shaking my hand in welcome, I told her the reason for my visit. "I'm sorry to have disturbed you ma'am, but I was looking for John Griffin Jr. Have you heard of him, or do you know which house is his?"

"Now, you don't have to call me ma'am, call me Mrs. Hamilton. Griffin? Griffin, you say."

"John Griffin, Jr," I said slowly, not sure if perhaps she was a little deaf.

"I know him well. He used to be mayor of New Windsor about six years ago. His house is that one over there." Mrs. Hamilton pointed to the house across the street from hers. "Seems there was a tragedy in the family recently…"

"Tragedy?" She had my full attention at the mere mention of the word since it may help shed some light on why I had inherited the old farmhouse.

"Yes," she said, shaking her head slowly, as she closed her front door, and shuffled over to a white wicker patio set on her wide front porch.

I followed and took a seat across from her. "Could you tell me what happened? You see, John and I were kids together; we used to play all kind of pretend games when I lived…"

"At Wakefield Road…the farm…I know it well." Mrs. Hamilton finished my sentence and seemed to know a great deal; this in itself had me very interested in what she had to say.

"How did you know?"

"When you're old, like I am, you read a lot, listen to the television, and gossip. But I remember when the Summers family used to live there, and I remember the tales of that wicked boy, William."

At the mention of his name, I sucked in my breath and stared with wide eyes at this elderly wonder. She had all but captured my very existence and I waited impatiently for her to continue.

"I heard through the grapevine that John's mother and father were hit by a train and killed instantly. You know, the tracks run right next to the house, and for some reason they were in an awfully big hurry to drive away. They must not have been looking where they was going and *wham!* It's a shame."

"Do you have a hunch as to why they were in a hurry to leave the house?"

"Now why would I know such a thing as that?"

She was playing dumb; I could tell by the way her eyes twinkled and how a slight smile played at the corners of her mouth.

"Well, *maybe* you heard through the grapevine the many opinions of others," I said in a suggestive way, raising my eyebrows high on my forehead and shaking my head. Urging her to speculate on the events of the train accident may not have been such a good idea; she was already starving for company and conversation and this might just be a perfect opportunity to make something up, tell me anything at all, just to keep me here listening.

"I did hear something, but it's so far fetched, you know, more like a Halloween story."

"Tell me anyway."

"They say the house was acting up," she whispered, while leaning close to my face.

"Acting up?"

"Strange happenings and such. Those folks didn't feel comfortable in their own house, they was afraid, you know, and they wanted out," she said, as she got up and pointed toward John Jr.'s house. "He didn't want it, that house, too many bad memories. He won't even clean out his parents' things."

I walked over and stood next to her on the edge of the porch. "Why not?" I said gazing over at his house and knowing my time to go over there and ask that very same question was coming up.

"I guess he 'fraid. His sister don't want nothin to do with that house; I guess that's why she moved to California just last week."

"Mrs. Hamilton, you've been a big help and it's been a pleasure speaking with you, but it think it's time for me to go over there and talk to John personally." I shook her soft, wrinkled hands and thanked her once more then turned and jogged across the street to John's house.

Chapter Five
The Unexpected Visitor

Five minutes later, I was ringing the doorbell of John's house and feeling a bit uncomfortable when no one answered right away. In fact, it took a lot of ringing and knocking for a good long while, peeking in the windows, even walking to the sides of the house and peering toward the backyard before someone finally opened the door.

"I said no more visitors!" a tall young man said, his voice filling with anger. His chubby cheeks were flushed red and his face was scrunched into a scowl, but all that changed the minute he saw me.

"Hi, John, remember me?" He squinted his eyes and seemed at a loss for words, and I could tell he was trying hard to remember who I was. I then held my watch up to my mouth and spoke into it, "Giant Robot, attack." I giggled and smiled. "Remember how we used to watch those old Japanese kid shows and then go outside and pretend?"

"Melissa? Melissa! Oh, my…I mean…look at you…wow, have you changed. What brings you here?" The words fell out of his mouth, and then he just stood there in the doorjamb staring at me, smiling and laughing.

"I came to ask about some paperwork that I've recently received. I was hoping you could answer some questions before I moved forward on this. Can I come in?"

"Oh, oh, sure, sure, come on in." John moved aside to make room for me to enter his beautiful, spacious home. It was an older home completely renovated; the freshly painted open and airy rooms gave the impression that the inside was bigger that it actually was, and decorated sparsely.

"Wow, this is so nice," I said.

"Thanks. I'm a bit confused as to how I could help you with paperwork, but come on out here in the kitchen and show it to me; there's lots of light and a great breeze from the sliding glass door when it's open." I followed him to a modern kitchen completely done in white with ivy and sunflower boarder and decorations. "Do you want something to drink?"

"Sure."

"How about iced tea?" he said showing me a large pitcher of iced tea and smiled, eager to please.

"That'll be great."

Once we had our cold drinks and sat at the table, I decided to dive right in. "John, I'm really sorry to hear about your parents."

His face took on a solemn look and he stared at his cup, then he snorted a laugh and looked up at me. "It was really the strangest thing. Those stupid train tracks have been there forever, and Mom and Dad go and get hit."

"It does sound a bit strange. They've lived there for years John, they knew about the train coming by once in a while, they would know to look before crossing. Do you think they were in a hurry to leave the house that day?" I chose my questions carefully, trying not to make him angry or upset in any way.

"Who knows what was going on?" John threw his hands up in the air in a gesture of giving up and leaned back in his chair, but I wasn't satisfied with his short answers.

"Didn't you go visit them, or talk to them over the phone?"

"Sure, when I had the time."

"When was the last time you were over there?"

"A week before the accident. Dad was trying to tell me something and I blew him off, I don't know, crazy old man talk, I guess." He wiped

24

his face with his hands and looked at me through his fingers. "What are you getting at, Melissa? Do you know something?"

"I only have a suspicion, but anything you can tell me may help shed light on my current mystery." I opened the manila envelope and pulled out the papers for him to review. "For some odd reason I've been willed your parents' house. I came to ask why this property didn't go to you, or your sister, Kathy. I'm not even a family member, and I really want to know why. I can't even pin the lawyer down to ask if he knows something."

He gave me a side-glance while looking over the deed to the old farmhouse then let out a heavy sigh and answered my question with a question. "Melissa, why was it that, after you moved, you always asked me and Kathy if we ever heard any strange noises in the house?"

"You'll laugh at me if I tell you," I warned, wagging a finger at him.

"I promise I won't, and if you tell me then it just might answer some questions I've had about that house for the past month." He was very sincere with his answer and the look in his eyes made me feel that I could trust him.

"When I lived there I always heard walking sounds coming from the attic that went on for the longest time. Then, one day, I encountered a spirit, a friendly spirit named Josh…"

"It had a name? Did it talk to you?"

"See, you're making fun…"

"No, I'm sorry, it just seems a bit far fetched—talking to spirits and all. Go on, tell your story and I won't laugh."

"Josh *did* talk to me, but *only* to me and no one else in my family. There was also another spirit, William, and he was the one making all the noise in the attic. Anyway, I discovered the truth about Josh's death, found the lost family fortune sealed up in the concrete wall in the basement, and captured the evil spirit of William in a crystal pyramid. Becky and I buried it out in the pasture, but I always had this weird feeling that William would find a way out—and take revenge in some type of way."

"You mean come back."

"Like find a way out of his prison and return to the house."

"Hmm, maybe that's what Dad was talking about," John said, stroking his stubbly chin with a forefinger. "He used go on and on about things being moved around in the house. At first he thought it was Mom pestering him, until they witnessed small pictures literally jumping from table to table in the living room, areas rugs wrinkling up so they would trip, the old hand pump out front would pump its own water, stuff like that. But the clincher was when Dad would wake up in the middle of the night hearing the whispered name of...the whispered name of..." His voice trailed off as he stared at the letter I received from the attorney.

"John, the whispered name of, who?" I said, giving his arm a little shake, I really wanted to hear his answer.

When he turned to look at me his face had gone pale, his hands began to tremble slightly, and his eyes were wide, "Melissa."

"What is it? What's wrong?"

"That was the name Dad heard. It was *your* name."

"Mine?" Now I began to worry. "Then maybe William *had* got out of that crystal."

"That sounds a bit far fetched, and I can't help but be very skeptical on that issue. Nevertheless, I'll level with you; Kathy and I didn't want that house. It was too old and needed way too much work, but the honest truth is that I won't go near that place, especially after Mom and Dad died so close to it."

"Not even to get their stuff?" I was shocked by his comment. It seemed to me that most kids would be waiting with their hands open to get hold of their parents' personal items. I watched John's face closely, as he sniffed and wiped a tear from his eye, and felt sorry for him. Unfortunately, our conversation wasn't shedding a great deal of light on why the house was awarded to me, other than John's idea that his dad willed it to me because he kept hearing my name whispered throughout the house.

"Did you or Kathy tell your parents to give the house to me?"

"I didn't, and I don't think Kathy thought of it; she was too busy getting ready to leave the state. I honestly feel that Dad gave the house to you because of hearing your name all the time. He must've thought the house wanted you back."

I ignored his creepy reasoning and pressed him with logical details. "Did he have a will?"

"I guess; but I'm not sure," John said, giving me a strange look.

"You don't know for certain if he had a will, so you don't have a copy, right?" He shook his head as I continued, and kept looking at me as if he was trying to figure out what I was thinking. "You haven't gone into the house since before they died so, how did this lawyer, William Anderson, get my name, address, and know to put a deed together willing me that house?" I thought for a moment then added, "Unless your parents went to him before the accident."

John shook his head and looked at the letter again. "Hey, wait a minute," he said, as an idea suddenly occurred to him, "there's no business at this address; it's a boarded up building. I should know since I was the mayor six years ago; I've kept up on all the officials and new business in town, and I've never heard of a lawyer named William Anderson, or a business going up at this address."

"What do you mean it's a boarded up building? I was just there this morning. Maybe you're thinking of a different building." I felt a little annoyed and scared at his comment.

"It's right next to the new printing company building, right?" It seemed that he wanted me to understand that he knew what he was talking about, possibly because I was giving him an odd look.

"Yes, but I went *in* the building. There were desks, phones, and computers, even a hot cup of coffee on the secretary's desk. However it was odd that no one was in the office when I arrived. I was there for a whole hour and nobody showed up, even though it clearly looked as though someone had been there. But you're saying it's a boarded up building, and I know what I saw just an hour ago. Of course, that would explain why I got so many strange looks from people that walked by." I took the paperwork from him and looked it over once more, then pulled the house key out of my pocket and stood up. "This is getting stranger by the minute and it seems that *somebody* wants me to have that house. I've been invited in. If you don't mind, I'm going over there and have a look around."

Chapter Six
The Old House

Twenty minutes later I pulled up in front of 27 Wakefield Road. John's parents had done a great deal of landscaping around the huge property. There was a gazebo in the front yard now, an in-ground swimming pool occupying the space where the garden used to be, and beautiful shrubs and flowers now lining the front porch and different areas of the huge front yard. I marveled at all the new windows with fancy woodwork, and fresh paint everywhere; John's dad even rebuilt the screened-in porch on the second floor outside Becky's old bedroom. He also installed a beautiful front door with a frosted oval glass window and modern storm door.

Wow, all this work must've cost a fortune. I wonder why John felt this house needed too much work? I hurried up the new flagstone sidewalk to the front door; the key slipping easily into place as I unlocked the door, opened it, and peeked inside.

What was once the kitchen was now a rather large sitting room, complete with Victorian furniture, heavy ivory drapes, and mounds of dusty pictures and knick-knacks. As I looked around, it became clear another reason why John Jr. may not want to come into the house and clear out his parents' things was because his mother was a collector. "It would take several huge moving vans to take all these things away," I mused. I continued to look around, walking from the sitting room into what was once the laundry room, but turned into a modern gourmet kitchen, and the spare bedroom now a beautiful dinning room. The only room on the first floor that wasn't changed was the old living room. There was now all new carpet and fancy wallpaper, but it was still the living room, where I used to watch all those cool kid shows like: *Wonder Woman, The Nancy Drew and Hardy Boys* series, and all the Saturday morning cartoon shows. I smiled to myself at the pleasant memories as I wandered back into the sitting room, and looked toward the curved stairway leading to the second floor.

"Wow," I spoke softly, "the second floor." While slowly approaching the bottom of the stairway, I thought back to when the second floor was where most of the scary haunting sounds could be heard.

"It's all gone now," I said to myself, taking one step at a time. "William is gone, hasn't come back, at least not that I know of, and there's no reason to be afraid." I tried to convince myself by recalling the day I tricked the disgusting spirit of William and trapped him in a pyramid-shaped crystal, and then with the help of my stepsister Becky, buried it out in the pasture. After that, the good spirit of Josh was finally able to rest in peace, the house was rid of creepy noises, and William was never heard from again.

I finally made my way to the second floor and stood at the beginning of the long hallway. Of course, it didn't seem as long as when I was thirteen, and was now covered with plush burgundy colored carpet; the walls faux painted ivory-gold. The three bedrooms on the right side of the hallway were all done up, each with its own decorated theme. Donna's rich tastes what they were, I didn't expect anything less. The large bathroom was now beautifully updated with Italian tile and mine, Becky's, and my parents' old bedrooms were all painted and nicely decorated. "I'm totally impressed," I said to myself. "Maybe I could sell this place and make some money after all."

I went into my old bedroom and it was clearly John Jr.'s at one time, lined with baseball posters and trophies, blue and red linens and bedspread, as well as furniture that looked as if it were meant for a boy. Lifting up one of the windows, I smiled and scanned the side view of the house; the apple trees I used to climb, the shed, and the long concrete walkway leading down to the barn and all the neat, old buildings that Becky and I loved to explore. Ahh, memories. My mom was always so worried about us falling through the old floorboards of that barn when we were in there swinging on ropes from one stack of hay bails to the next, jumping from the hay loft, or just plain goofing around, but what she should've been more afraid of was our being sucked up by a sink hole. The pasture was full of fairly large sinkholes and as I gazed out over it I noticed some of them were the same size as they were eight years ago, and now smaller ones had begun to develop.

Sinkholes were nothing to fool around with; one could open up the ground from under your feet and you could fall deep, possibly being crushed by rocks, or smothered by dirt. Years ago, a huge sink hole opened up on the main highway that passed by Wakefield Road and three cars fell in, killing the drivers, but the road was fixed and nothing more was done about the old farm that contained the biggest threat of sinkholes on its land. Becky and I never worried about the problem, we just loved going out to the pasture to wade in the stream and catch minnows, and always steered clear of the sinkholes, or of any ditches or gullies signaling the start of one, no matter what danger there might have been.

Closing the window, I sat on the edge of the bed and suddenly got a strange notion. "Josh! Josh are you here? It's me, Melissa." I looked around the room, as if I were expecting someone to appear, and I almost hoped to see an indentation in the bedspread or feel a weight pressing against me. However, when nothing happened, I got up and snickered, shaking my head, and started for the end of the hallway. "Boy, what a dope," I mused, and felt a bit annoyed at myself for thinking that the spirit of Josh would automatically come back just because I was here in this house again.

I made my way to the attic door and stood staring at it for a moment, noticing the bent nails Becky hammered around the doorjamb so William wouldn't get out; the chipped wood around the door, and the old latch lock was now rusty with the black paint peeling away. My courage having grown since I first came upstairs, I was convinced there was nothing to be afraid of—well, almost convinced. Flashes of memories came to mind repeatedly, my hand shaking as it went for the latch lock.

Boom! Boom!

The sound came from downstairs; and the suddenness made me jump and hastily withdraw my hand from opening the attic door.

I ran down the stairs to the sitting room and on to the front door. No one was there. "That's funny, I know I heard a loud noise," I muttered, going to the windows in the living room and looking out. My car was the only one in the driveway, and it didn't look as if someone had walked up and banged on the front door. *Maybe someone is at the large side door*, I thought as I went outside and rounded the long porch. The sun was bright and the day was warming up, and I totally forgot I should get to work soon before half the workday was gone. I walked around the back of the house and noticed nothing either unusual or out of place, and it looked as if no one was around to bang on the door. I continued to walk around the house, passing the small back porch and the old smokehouse, however as I rounded the opposite side of the house a tingle of alarm ran up my spine at the sight of the cellar doors laying wide open.

"I wonder how long this has been open?" I said, taking a few steps down into the dark and then pausing. "Hello? Is anybody down here?" I took a few more steps and stopping one step away from the dirt basement floor, sat down.

Boom! Boom!

The sound echoed throughout the basement loud enough that the old copper pipes jiggled. *Must be air in the pipes, or road workers hitting the piping that these connect to somewhere*, I thought, but continued to sit on the bottom step and peer into the dark basement. Immediately I looked over to the left, and noticed the spot where Becky and I uncovered the hidden jewelry William stole and sealed up in the wall. Though the wall still had dips and chips left from where we chiseled plaster and brick away, and then tried our best to seal the hole up again, it was still a constant reminder of all the things that scared me about this place. When the booming sounds didn't happen again for quite a while,

I stood up, walked back up the steps, closed up the basement and secured the old wooden doors.

Feeling quite happy that I had myself a renovated eighteenth century house and was going to sell it for a large sum of money, I started walking away from the basement side of the house, but when a sudden gust of wind whipped around me and blew fallen leaves around my feet I froze in place. I couldn't understand why I stopped; it was like I was a puppet and the person pulling the strings wouldn't let me walk to my car. Then I heard a new sound. "Melissa," it said in a deep, breathy, gurgling voice, which seemed to come up from the ground and circle around me. My eyes widened and my breath quickened, I knew that voice, it was one that I would never forget—William.

Chapter Seven
A Grave Mistake

Shaking myself free of the sudden terror filling my very soul I broke into a run. Dashing for my navy blue Volvo, I fumbled frantically for the car keys, pulled them out of my pocketbook, and struggled to get the car started. I revved the engine and peered through the windshield toward the house, half expecting William to burst up out of the ground and come after me, and half expecting to hear his voice in my car. When neither happened I calmed down a bit and stared at the wonderful old house once more, and that's when I noticed that the front door was wide open. That must've happened when I went to investigate the booming noise.

"Oh, no," I moaned, knowing full well that I couldn't leave with the door open; anyone could go in and raid the place, or vandalize it, and I was sure the gossip of how disrespectful and irresponsible I was to leave the house unsecured would spread all the way to Mrs. Hamilton. "Well, I can't have the old ladies talking bad about me," I mused. "I guess I have to suck it up and go lock the front door."

I turned off the car, got out, took a deep breath, and marched up the front walk in a very determined fashion. "All I have to do is lock the door," I said to myself, "the key must still be in the knob, I don't have to go inside, just lock it, take the key, and get to work." I slowed my pace as I approached the front door that had drifted wide open, and cautiously reached for the knob. The key was still in the lock as I cautiously peered in and, not wanting to step too far inside, I strained to reach for the doorknob; pushing on the hinged-edge of the door to make it drift closed again. This little trick wasn't working, however, and I reluctantly stepped inside and grabbed for the key, only to have it fly out of the knob and disappear into the house.

I stared helplessly after the key, as my fear mounted, and my heart pounded hard inside my chest. "I don't care," I called out into the house, "I'm not coming in after the key. Keep it!"

I fumbled with the knob to make sure it wasn't locked, shut the door, and ran for my car once more. *It'll be fine until I get a spare key from John, that is, if he has a key,* I thought, while getting into my Volvo.

I couldn't be worried about the house not being properly locked; the door was shut and it appeared perfectly fine. I pushed the thought from my mind, and turned the key—the car wouldn't start.

"Oh, no," I whined. "Don't do this. You were running just a minute ago." I pumped the gas pedal and turned the key again, it still wouldn't start. "Come on!" Panic seized me and I tried over and over to get the car to start so I could get away from this place, but no response. I sat behind the wheel for a moment, staring at the house and looking up at the attic window, then whipped out my cell phone and called work.

"Rachel? Hi, this is Melissa Grey. Could you please tell Mr. McDermond that I'll be later than expected…yes…he knows that I went to a lawyer's office this morning to check out a house that I inherited and now it seems my car is dead…I mean, won't start." I tried my best to explain my situation without giving too much detail away. Rachel was a good receptionist, but way too nosy and had a bad habit of telling other people's business to the whole office. I really didn't want anyone to know about the situation I was now in, but deep in my heart, I knew there was one person I should be calling in particular, so I tried to finish up the conversation with Rachel. "Are you sure you got all the information correct, and you'll pass the message on? Okay…thanks…bye."

As soon as I hung up with our receptionist, I pushed speed dial and called Becky.

"Hello?"

"Becky, I'm so glad I got hold of you." The tone of my voice rose and I suddenly felt like I was going to cry.

"Melissa, what's wrong? Are you okay?"

"I'm at the old house…"

"What?" Now her voice went up.

"You know, the old house, the one we used to live in, in New Windsor," I said.

"I know what you mean, but why are you there?"

I quickly recited the happenings from the moment I got the mysterious letter to the key whisking away through the house. "And now my car won't start. I don't know what to do."

"Don't freak out just yet…"

"Too late. And Becky?"

"Yeah?"

"I heard William's voice. He was whispering my name and it sounded like it was coming from the ground. I first heard it when I threw that letter from the lawyer in the trash at work, and I heard it again, just a few minutes ago. I hate to say it, but I think he's come back somehow; and if not, then he's up to some new haunting tricks."

"Look, just chill, okay? I'll call the home office and tell them I'm going off line for the rest of the day due to a family emergency, and I'll come get you." It was lucky for me that Becky worked from home as a troubleshooter technician for a very large computer company; all her smarts, that I hated so much as a kid, finally paid off.

"There's something you have to know, Becky…"

"What? You're breaking up, Melissa." She shouted into the phone "The phone's breaking up…I can't hear you…"

Becky kept shouting into the phone that she couldn't hear me, yet I could hear her perfectly fine, and I suspected the spirit of William was somehow interfering with the cell phone reception. Finally, the line went dead and I was alone. I looked at the phone in disgust and dropped it into my purse, while sinking back into the driver's seat. *Would Becky make it here before something else happened? Would I have to leave my car here? What if Becky got here and William trapped her somehow?* While all these crazy questions ran through my mind, I happened to look up and noticed that the front door to the house was open again.

Chapter Eight
The Sink Hole

"I am *not* going to close that stupid door again," I mumbled to myself, sitting very still and gripping the steering wheel. But the more I stared at the front door hanging wide open, the more it bothered me. *This has to be the work of William.* I was totally convinced William had come back to take revenge on me for trapping him in that crystal and burying him in the ground, there didn't seem to be any other logical explanation.

During the time I had lived here, I read tons of books on ghosts, hauntings, poltergeists, and things of that nature. Over the past few years I became extremely interested in television shows, movies, and more scientific books on spooks—so I could get a better understanding of what I went through as a thirteen-year-old and possibly how best to deal with those memories years later. All this knowledge made me believe my William theory was correct—and nothing was going to change my mind.

Yet here I was, stuck at the old house, the one place I left the spirit of William, and the one place where he seemed to have an advantage over me. I wasn't sure how, but my gut feeling told me *he* swiped the key out of the doorknob and kept opening the front door, inviting me to my doom. Well, I wasn't accomplishing anything just sitting in my car and I had no idea how long it would take Becky to pick me up; I would feel much better if I had some company, maybe at one of the neighbors.

I got out of my car and looked around at my options. The nearest neighbor, both elderly people, from what I remember as a child, was a half-mile away and I would have to walk. At the moment, walking didn't seem like a bad idea; anything was better than sitting here for an hour or more with the open door and the voice of William taunting me.

I started walking down the quarter-mile stone and dirt driveway, with the thought of heading towards the house that used to belong to Miss Summers. I wasn't sure if she still lived there, or if she was even alive, but it just felt good knowing I could go to someone who would understand my situation and wouldn't mind if I hung out until my stepsister got here. Even though I had made up my mind not to worry about the house, I kept looking over my shoulder at the front door, lazily closing part way and then drifting open repeatedly, as if moved by a breeze. *I'm not going to worry about that door*, I thought again, in a very determined fashion. I wasn't completely stupid and there was no way I'd fall for a simple-minded trick like rushing in to the house just to close the door.

Suddenly, the ground began to tremble; the vibrations were subtle, yet firm and I stopped thinking about where I was going and stared at the driveway. *What was it—an earthquake—maybe the train? Nah, the train never vibrated the ground like this!* My string of questions were answered as several tiny, volcano-shaped mounds of dirt sprung up just a few feet in front of me.

"What the heck?"

I took a few cautious steps closer to one of the mounds and noticed that there was an opening at the top, like an ant hill, but bigger, and what suddenly climbed out of the hole wasn't an ant—it was a furry black spider.

The eight-legged creature squeezed its large bulbous body out of the small opening, shook the dirt from itself, and then turned to face me. My eyes widened and my whole body trembled with fear at the sight of this spider that was bigger than my hand. I took a step backward as it crawled slowly toward me, moving its fangs. Then, from out of the other mounds, more spiders emerged, all the same size as the first, each one just as black and furry as the next, and in an instant, a swarm of them spread across the whole driveway and out into the yard—and now blocking my path.

The first spider that climbed out of the dirt took a few more slow paces forward and I felt my heartbeat quicken, and the cold hand of fear tighten around my throat. I had to put some distance between this menace and me, while not freaking out in the process. And while I was thinking of a plan on how to do this, a few of the other spiders crawled forward as well, moving their fangs as clear, thick fluid began to drip from what I suspected was their mouths. *This doesn't look good!* I thought, and walked backwards a little faster; the tiny loose stones of the driveway making me stumble, but I did not fall. The spiders advanced, a wave of furry black bodies massing together, forming an arc, as if to surround me, crawling faster in an effort to match my strides. Not being able to take it anymore, I panicked and screamed as loud as I could. I turned and ran with all my might toward the house with the spiders in hot pursuit.

My first thought was to burst through the open front door and shut myself inside, but that's just what William would want me to do. No, I had to do something else—and fast! I cut across the lawn, dodged the low branches of the huge Maple tree in front of the house, and headed for the barn. The thunder of the many-legged creatures echoed all around the old farm, and they quickly caught up with me as I reached the barn door; straining with all my might to slide the weather worn door open, but the metal wheels were rusted and wouldn't budge. Abandoning that idea, I instead ran toward the chicken yard in hope of being able to climb up on some of the low buildings. That idea was foiled as a sea of spiders cut around the swimming pool and came at me from the left.

I doubled back toward the barn, thinking I could get in through the huge doors that lead to the hayloft, but spiders were there waiting for me, blocking the doors and lifting their front legs as if to attack. However, they weren't attacking, at least not yet, and I stood my ground, trying to catch my breath and get a fix on where all the spiders were located. Several had climbed up on the roof of the barn, while others were up in the old Locust trees lining the chicken yard and storage buildings; spinning webs right above me high up in the branches. The group of spiders that came from the chicken yard were coming up behind me at such a fast pace my only option was to head back toward the house.

"This is nuts," I puffed, running through a small opening the spiders left unattended, while trying to come at me from the right. My legs ached from running and a cramp tightened up on my left side, but I couldn't stop, if I did, I would be spider food. I broke past the mass swarming all around me, screaming as a few spiders jumped at me from the barn roof; the ones in the tree tops descended from their webbing and were inches from my head, but I dodged each one as I used my last bit of energy to head for the house.

I reached the basement doors before any of the spiders. With trembling fingers, I unlatched the doors and flung them wide open, then ran down the concrete steps into the musty dankness of the basement. I didn't close the doors because I was afraid of being shut in the dark basement alone and not being able to see if the spiders were coming in after me.

Moments passed, and no spiders showed their ugly, furry faces at the top of the steps. I struggled with the idea of going back up the concrete steps and shutting the doors, but I *knew* those spiders were up there waiting for me. So, I waited, pacing nervously in place and never taking my eyes away from the opened doors. From where I stood, I could see sun, sky, and the tops of apple trees, but no spiders. *Where were they? What was going on?*

Then another horrible thought came to mind. The entire basement floor was nothing but dirt and I silently worried that the spiders would burrow up through the ground and come after me that way. Of course, to me that seemed like too much work, I mean, why do that when the doors were sitting wide open with nothing to stop them?

"This isn't right," I nervously whispered, my stomach knotting as I moved toward the basement steps, but I stopped in mid-step as a lone spider appeared at the top. I just stood there, staring at it, and it was just staring at me. Then, out of the silence, came a deep rumbling, and the ground beneath my feet began to pitch and sway, causing me to lose my balance and fall to the dirt floor. I grabbed the dirt with my hands, as if doing so would keep me steady, and I kept trying to stand up, only to be tossed back down to the ground.

"Stop it! Stop it!" I said, but to whom, I wasn't sure. All I knew was that I wanted to scream at someone, to make this whole thing go away.

Then, to make matters worse, the ground beneath me started spinning, swirling around like a whirlpool, with me inching toward the ever-sinking middle. Trying to steady myself wasn't going to work and I felt as if I was on a record player with no way off, but when the center of the vortex dropped and an actual funnel formed, I knew I had to do something fast. I gathered my strength and lunged for the bottom of the concrete steps, but my fingers missed them by mere inches. The hole forming in the ground was getting wider and deeper and I felt my legs getting caught in the suction. I clawed wildly at the edge of the hole, kicking and struggling to free myself of this horrible fate, but the sinkhole just got wider and I finally lost my grip.

"No! No! Help me, someone, help me!" Dirt got in my mouth and eyes as I threw back my head and screamed as loud as I could, but no matter what I did I was dragged into the center of the sinkhole and everything suddenly went black.

Chapter Nine
On Forbidden Ground

My head was spinning and my body aching as I lay half buried, in a pile of dirt and stone. I couldn't move at first, so I just lie on my back very still, letting my eyes adjust to the darkness which mixed with the light filtered through the hole from which I fell. The hole above me was very wide and perfectly round, covering most of the basement floor before it reached the many rooms that went under the entire house, and from what I could make out, I was at least fifteen feet below ground. Even though it hurt to do so, I lifted my head and looked around, propping myself up on an elbow and brushing some dirt off my stomach and chest with my free hand.

The interior of the sinkhole was smooth, with no rocks sticking out of the wall, natural ledges of dirt, or roots from trees to climb. The faint light from the hole above allowed me to see that not only was I at the bottom of a very unusual sinkhole, but a tunnel as well, as tall as it was wide, and the darkness extending into the tunnel made it difficult to tell just how deep it was. Most sinkholes don't drop into an open tunnel; the ground normally dropped because of weak lime stone bedrock and sediments caused by underground water and erosion. The bottom opening up into this tunnel raised suspicions on how it actually formed.

"Hmm, I had no idea there was a tunnel under the farm," I said, brushing more dirt from my clothes and hair. My head wasn't reeling anymore and despite my back aching, I knew I had to stand. Wiggling my legs free of more dirt, I drew my legs under me and tried rise.

"Arrgh!"

My right ankle throbbed and a stab of pain shot up my leg. I gripped my leg, bit my lower lip and tried not to cry, but the pain was horrible.

"Now what am I going to do with a twisted ankle?" I softly sobbed.

"Howww does it feeeelll?" A deep, whispery voice, sounding as if someone was gurgling mud echoed off the walls.

My stomach tightened and a wave of fear washed over me because I knew to whom that voice belonged—William. Ignoring the question, I scooted over to the wall to steady myself, and then struggled to a standing position and scanned the darkness. He was here—somewhere—in the dirt walls, under the ground, in the air…I wasn't sure…but I just *knew* he was lurking somewhere close by.

"Painnnnn…feeelll painnn, toooo, ha, ha, ha…"

What the heck is he talking about? He can't feel pain—he's dead! However, one thing was certain, William was watching me. He knew I was hurt and in pain, but where was he? I looked all around, hopping in place on one foot, and strained my eyes to see further down the tunnel. It was so dark down there I was afraid to leave the security of the little bit of light shining down on me from the hole.

"Help!" I shouted up through the opening, "Becky, you here yet? Help, down here, help!" Even though there was no response, I listened for any type of sound; a car pulling into the driveway, the door of the house closing, someone calling for me…anything, but I heard nothing. *It's gotta be noon by now*, I thought, *I should've been to work an hour ago. Boy, Mr. McDermond is going to yell at me, that is, if I ever get out of here.* I leaned heavily against the dirt wall and considered my options for getting out of this mess. *Well, I can't climb up, especially with a twisted ankle, Becky's not here and I don't know when she'll show up, and this light won't last forever; it'll get dark in a few hours.* If only I hadn't left my cell phone in the car, I could call for help.

Even though I didn't want to do it, I knew that I had to hobble down the tunnel and see if there was another way out. I pushed off from the dirt wall and put too much weight on my bad ankle, causing me to scream out in pain.

"There's got to be something I can use to lean on."

Dropping down on my knees, I crawled around in the dirt until I found a branch; crooked but thick and almost the perfect height, I only had to bend over a little bit once it was nestled under my arm. Although the branch cut into my armpit, it wasn't so bad that I couldn't deal with it as I slowly made my way down into the dark tunnel.

Dank musty odors of dirt and moisture surrounded me as I carefully felt my way down the tunnel, using my free hand and the branch as my guide. The walls and the ground were beginning to get muddy, and I soon recognized the sound of trickling water.

"If there's water up ahead, that must mean part of the stream that runs through the pasture is now below ground," I mumbled. "And if it's still flowing then that means there's a way out for the water, which means a way out for me."

I hobbled a little faster, but stopped short when I heard my name coming in whispered waves from all around. It echoed off the walls, gurgled up from under my feet, and got lost in the darkness further down the tunnel.

"Cut it out, William," I said in a very angry tone. "You're not going to get the better of me."

There was a long, unnerving silence, but I stayed very still, quieting my breathing, and listening intently for any sounds. At first there was nothing, no sound, no movement, no nothing, but all of that changed when I noticed the muddy, dirt walls on either side of me begin to run, as if melting, and start to form a thickness around my feet.

Chapter Ten
Trapped

Lifting my walking stick out of the mud was tougher than I had imagined for it became heavy and hard like cement, in a matter of moments.

"Yessss, I wiiilll," William gurgled, finally responding to my last statement, then ended with a cruel chuckle.

I tried my best to hobble away through the mud, pulled my unhurt foot out of the soupy sludge with a disgusting slurp, and almost lost my shoe in the process. With a constant string of "Owws" mixed with a lot of whining due to my twisted ankle, I managed to move forward, and far enough away, from the built up mud. I turned around and looked at the wall forming behind me.

"Oh, my…it would've been up to my knees by now, if I wouldn't have moved," I said, still in disbelief at how fast the mud was forming a barrier between me and the only opening I knew. *If Becky showed up, she would never know where I was. What am I going to do?*

Just at that moment, as if reading my mind, the dirt ceiling, right above where the mud was running, began to crumble, spewing dust and dirt into the air and making it very hard to breathe, showering down non-stop until the entire entry was blocked.

"Great!" I grumbled, waving away clouds of dust and coughing.

Now I was really stuck and had no choice but to continue down the dark tunnel. William had me where he wanted me, and having to hobble around on one foot left me very defenseless, but I wasn't going to give up. I turned around and continued to feel my way down the tunnel, following the sound of running water.

I could only imagine that I was somewhere under the pasture, perhaps close to the wide and twisting stream that Becky and I loved to wade in when we were kids. I knew from listening to my stepdad that sinkholes had a connection with water flowing under and through limestone and weak underground structures. Being a pipeline engineer, he knew a lot about geology. He had to, because if he drilled a hole for laying pipe and the ground wasn't stable, it would cause major problems for the construction workers. I couldn't figure out how I actually remembered such a thing, normally I didn't listen to my parents' conversations, but right now, I was glad I retained that type of information; it could be helpful.

My hearing became more accordant to my surroundings, since I couldn't see. I continued to plod and grope my way down the dark tunnel, shivering in the cold, and feeling dirty and uncomfortable. The dirt wall I had been touching suddenly became very wet, and I followed the path of water as it ran down in a fast paced trickle, pooled at my feet, and continued down the tunnel. Still feeling along with my hand, I followed the trickle of water back up the wall in the hopes of finding its source. Where water ran out there had to be a source from up above, which could be an escape.

I patted the wall. "The opening has to be here," I said, breathing hard and straining to follow the water, and I reached as far up the dirt wall as my height would allow. I tried to adjust my eyes in the dark and barely caught a glimpse of a speck of light seeping in through a pinhole opening from above. "Yes!" I felt triumph and leaned all my weight against the dirt wall, as I used the end of the walking stick to prod the hole bigger.

Shoving the stick into the hole and twisting it around made the opening bigger, but it also let in more water. The good thing was it also let in a little more light, and revealed the water was running into a small sinkhole that filtered into the tunnel.

"Okay, I can't get out that way," I decided, while getting the stick up under my arm once again and stepping away from the wall. "Well, this water's going somewhere, and if I follow it I may find the exit it's using."

What comes in has to go out, that's what my mother used to say, and as I followed what I could see of the running water it was evident that the trickle was gaining in size and speed, becoming wider and deeper. And as the water grew the tunnel shrank, the ceiling getting lower, making it hard for me to use the walking stick. I had to get lower, and lower, crawling on my hands and knees with the stick gripped in my left hand and dragging my hurt foot. I was filthy from head to toe, and the dank, musty smell of the dirt walls filled my lungs with every moan and groan of each breath, until I felt the dirt in my mouth, under my nails, in my shoes and hair.

"Melissa," a deep whispered voice erupted from behind me.

"Melissa." Now it sounded like it was in front of me!

During this whole time I didn't completely forget about William, I knew he was somewhere in this tunnel, watching me, following my every move, and possibly planning surprises or attacks. He already showed he was powerful again by the way he made the tunnel close up, and now he was making his presence known again.

I crawled faster. "I have to get out of this tight spot," I mumbled.

"Melllisssaaaaa." My name was resounding all around me—close to my legs, right in my face, under me, above me, and in my head. The louder and closer it got, the faster I moved, trudging across the pasty dirt floor, the flowing water so close to my right that several times I put my hand in it. When was this tunnel going to open up again?

"How does it feeeelll?"

"Shut up, William!"

"Down in the ground…"

"You're already dead, I'm not!"

His questions were taunting me and getting on my nerves; but because of them, I imagined that the tightening of the tunnel was also his work. He wanted me to see how it felt to be underground, trapped, buried as I did him.

When his echoing voice died down, I stopped. Breathing hard, feeling closed in and buried alive, I slowly slid my right leg under my belly, fighting the pain that shot up my leg from the hurt ankle, and wiped tears from my eyes. Just when I thought I could rest a moment and let the pain subside, a hand punched its way through the floor next to my right leg. The grimy claw-like, maggot-covered hand grasped the air at first, and then reached for my leg. I let out a shrill scream as it latched on, digging its dirty fingernails into my thigh. Without a second to lose, I swatted at the hand in a crazy madman-type of way; punching it with my right hand, screaming as it finally let go and didn't stop pounding on it until it went back into the ground.

Whimpering over the cuts on my leg, I decided that now would not be the time to stop, and continued dragging myself, and the walking stick, through the tight tunnel. But once again, the disgusting hand shot out of the ground, this time where I had just been, and latched onto my left foot. The surprise attack startled me, and I screamed but didn't slow my progress as I pulled my foot away from the hand before it had a chance to dig its mangy nails into my skin once more. My heart pounded and my breath came in short gasps as I quickened my pace, scooting along the tight dirt tunnel, inching closer to the water until my pants and shoes got wet. The flow of water was now deep and swift enough to be considered a stream and I anxiously followed it, hoping that it would eventually lead me out of this horrible situation.

The hand kept plaguing me, popping out of the ceiling and grabbing my hair, and then coming out of the side of the tunnel my left side was plastered against, and gouged my skin until I was able to slide away. I couldn't take it much longer; the attacks were becoming quicker and more violent with the hand ripping at my flesh anyway it could and leaving marks in areas that I couldn't see in the dark, but could feel the heat from the pain they caused.

Finally the tunnel was becoming wider and I was able to get up on my knees and crawl a few paces, but not before a hideous face protruded from the dirt ceiling directly in front of me. Eyes barely in their sockets; teeth as well as lips and half the face rotted away, it stretched down lower, like a snake from a tree limb, hovering just inches from my face. It was William looking worse now than what he did when he emerged from the attic eight years ago, and he hissed and snapped at me like a crazed rabid dog. I was determined to get past him and brought the walking stick up, hitting the face with the bunt end several times as hard as I could. He howled an ear splitting, spine tingling yell, then growled until my attacks made him think better of bothering me, and the face slowly receded back into the dirt ceiling.

Chapter Eleven
The Confrontation

Once the disgusting face was gone, I didn't waste any more time crawling as fast as I could until the tunnel gave way and opened up into a small cavern. Light streaming in through small holes in the ceiling made seeing much easier. The little stream I had been following connected with a much larger and strong flowing stream that separated the landmass I stood on from one on the other side. The stream then continued to my right, and seemed to be heading toward what looked like more light.

"Maybe that's a way out," I said in a hopeful tone.

I pulled myself up to a standing position and got the walking stick under my arm once more, but not before staggering and crying out in pain due to my ankle. It was very swollen now; I could tell by how extremely tight my foot was inside my shoe. Not only did I have to deal with the messed up ankle, but now I had several cuts and gouges because of William's attacks. I looked at my left side and right leg, both had two or three marks, that I could distinguish through my clothes, and blood was oozing from wounds beneath the rips in the material. They were sore already and had the feeling of being puffy; so now I worried about infection, or possibly poison.

Walking was now more of a chore than it was earlier, and my whole body felt beaten to a pulp, but I couldn't stop, I had to make my way further down the tunnel toward the light and see if there was an opening I could crawl out through. The little streams of light seeping in through the ceiling made it easy to see much of the cavern. I shuffled closer to the embankment of the wide stream and gazed at the bit of dirt and pebble covered land on the other side, scanning the dirt walls and dark recesses in case there was an opening that I didn't want to overlook.

Movement on the darkest part of the dirt floor caught my eye right away. It started small at first, like a wisp of air blowing dust over a dry and parched desert, and then increased; the ground bubbling, gurgling, and popping so fast I thought it was going to explode. Instead, the trembling earth parted slightly and the same clawed hand which attacked me earlier emerged, but this time it was accompanied by an arm and a head and then, as if on a slow moving elevator, the entire corpse of William rose up out of the ground. He stood very still with his back to me, until he was completely out of the dirt then lowered his hand.

I stared with my mouth hanging open, totally in shock at the reality that he really had escaped out of the crystal after all. How he did it, I wasn't sure, but it was obvious that not only was Mrs. Moore's idea not fool proof, but that William's evil power was stronger than I imagined. My mind whirled at the idea that I was now deep underground, hurt and battered, barely able to get around let alone fight for my life, and trapped with a crazed spirit now in the morbid solid form of a walking corpse. Not only that, but this corpse had a grudge against me and I didn't think our meeting was going to be a gentle slap on the wrist. He was bent on revenge for defeating him, trapping him in the crystal and burying it out in the pasture, while setting Josh free to rest in peace.

I felt my heart pound wildly and a knot tighten in my stomach, as I waited for him to turn around. *Maybe I shouldn't wait? Maybe I should head toward the light and not give William a chance to say anything to me? Maybe he wouldn't notice with his back turned?*

"Melissa," William said in the same deep, gravelly voice I heard the day I trapped him in the crystal eight years ago—the sound of it sending shock waves of fear racing up my spine, forcing me to hold my position.

He slowly turned his head and looked at me from over his right shoulder. "We meet at last, you living piece of filth!" He spat the words out as he turned the rest of his body to face me.

"I didn't call *you* names." Even though my mouth was dry, I managed to squeak out the words.

Ignoring my comment, William took a step toward the embankment of his side of the wide stream. "Welcome to my world," he said, gesturing with his left hand, the one with a little bit of flesh hanging loose around the bone.

"Was all of this," I said as I glanced around quickly with my eyes, "your idea...your scheming?"

"Yessss," he hissed, his gnarled lips fluttering slightly as he spoke. "The illusions were more than your mortal mind could comprehend."

"What illusions?"

"I created it all, everything..."

"Everything?" Then my mind reflected back to what John had told me about the office building. "I guess the lawyer's office was fake, huh?"

"Yesss. All illusions to lure you here."

"You set me up." I hobbled a few paces toward the tunnel, wanting to get closer to a possible exit and put distance between us.

If the office was an illusion then the letter must've been an illusion, even though I felt it, held it in my hands. I didn't want to ask how he managed the secretary's voice when I called the fake office. No wonder people were looking at me as if I was a lunatic when I went into the building. To me it looked like a normal office, but anyone else could see it for what it really was. When I didn't ask him any further questions, he continued to gloat about how he had the upper hand.

"How did you like my spiders?" Placing his hands on his bony hips, he tossed his head back, which made the bones in his neck crack, while releasing a cruel chuckle.

"*Those* were illusions, too?" Now I felt really stupid for being fooled but, at the time, the spiders seemed very real. Then another horrible thought occurred to me; he had the power to get into my mind, to make me believe whatever he wanted. This wasn't good. How would

I be able to defend myself against a sinister mind game? Moreover, if the spiders were just a trick to get me into the basement, then I wonder what else he did to trick me. How far could his powers reach?

"There's no way out," William gurgled in an angry tone, pointing at the tunnel entrance toward which I was slowly making my way.

"You, ah, you thought of everything, didn't you, William?" I fumbled with my words, anxious to keep him bragging, while I slowly shuffled toward the way out of the cavern. I had an idea that if he were too busy talking he wouldn't be able to concentrate his illusion powers on my mind. I wasn't sure if it would work, but it was worth a try. "You've gotten pretty powerful, huh?"

"Limitless. Unlike you, your puny mind can't handle what I can dish out."

"It's always about you, isn't it? What did you do to the man and woman that used to live in the house? Tell me. What did you do to make them run right into the path of a train?" I suddenly felt both brave and angry. I wanted to know the truth about what happened to John and Donna. I stopped my sideways shuffle toward the escape route and turned to face him, the light streaming through the ceiling made it easier to see him fully.

"They didn't see or hear the train. But they did see the spiders," he sniggered and took two more steps toward me, moving around the light streams.

"You're evil, William! How could you?"

"Because I wanted you back, Melissa," he said, pointing a bony finger at me and scowling. "I wanted you back here—forever."

"What's done is done. It's over, let it go."

"You trapped me in that crystal and buried it! Buried *me*! You had no intentions of ever letting me out!" William screamed. He thrashed his torn and decaying arms wildly about while approaching me from the far side of the cavern.

My eyes widened in terror as the rotting corpse rushed at me. I had to get moving fast! He may be falling apart, but that wasn't stopping him from moving across the dirt floor quickly. Panic gripped my heart, as I picked up my swollen ankle and hopped on one foot toward the lighted tunnel, using the stick to urge myself forward. I had to hurry, he was almost to the water; my breath came in short gasps as I kept looking over my shoulder at the approaching carcass and that's when I tripped and fell flat on my face. The impact hurt, but I couldn't stop. I scrambled in place, rushing to get up, to get away, and I turned over on my back just in time to see him jump the stream.

Chapter Twelve
A Near Miss

William let out a high pitched shriek, bounding over the swift flowing stream and landing on the bank close to me with a vibrating thud. With his arms raised, poised to strike, he screamed once more and came at me with a menacing growl. I backed away, the smell of his rotting body becoming overwhelming the closer he got, and winced at the idea of his gnarled hands wrapping around my neck, or his gross fingers gouging out my eyes. I had to get up, but I couldn't take my eyes off of him as he took one slow step at a time toward me, pacing himself like a hunter stalking his prey. I inched backward until I came in contact with the dirt wall and the entrance I had been working toward was to my right. William walked closer; his body making a sick squishy sound with every step, the stench of his rotting corpse wafting in my direction was enough to make me want to throw up, and he grinned at me, though the one side of his face was practically rotted away.

Picking up my walking stick, I aimed it at him, ready to defend myself and run it through his juicy innards if I had to. As his gaze fell on the stick, William recognized my intentions, and he snarled as he stepped closer, and then crouched, like a tiger ready to pounce. With my back against the dirt wall, I started to rise to my feet, standing on my good foot and slowly inching up, but keeping the stick pointed at him.

Unable to wait any longer for his moment of triumph, he sprang forward, dashing through a beam of sunlight that had been separating us, then abruptly halted and screamed at the top of his lungs. He swat at the sunlight with bony arms, trying to protect his sunken, rotting eyes. Instantly, he realized it wasn't working and screamed even more at the sight of steam rising up from different parts of his body. He smacked at the wisps of vapor, which seemed to be getting thicker as more spouted on his head, back, and legs. Now he was frantic, dancing in place while continuously trying to pat out the overwhelming steam.

By this time, I had rose to my full height and got the walking stick back under my arm. If William was going to explode, or something of that nature, I wanted to put as much distance between us as possible, and shuffled just inside the opening of the new tunnel. I watched from the safety of the tunnel mouth as he continued his spastic display, until he couldn't take it any more and whirled around, vanishing into the ground with a quick sucking motion.

I stood there, staring at the spot where he was just a moment ago, and felt a bit dumbfounded at what just happened. *William's not dead, that's for sure,* I thought, *but he's definitely hurt. So, he returned to the place where he's been the past eight years. But for how long; just until he regains his strength, or he thinks of a new plan for attacking me?* Either way, I didn't want to find out. I turned and hobbled toward the light within the tunnel that beckoned me.

Chapter Thirteen
An Alternate Route

I lumbered along the tunnel, the stream with a small embankment next to it now on my left. I stayed to the right, following a three foot wide strip of dirt that got narrow then wide again based on the ever-changing stream. I quickly approached the first curve in the tunnel walls and saw light pouring down from an opening above. My heart skipped a beat as I rushed around the curve. *This could be a way out*, I thought and desperately hoped I was right. Unfortunately, the sunlight was coming in from a small hole in the top of the tunnel; too small to squeeze through and too high up for me to reach. I surveyed the walls around me, all of which were completely smooth, with no rocks or vines sticking out to climb. So still trapped under ground, I submitted to this small defeat and continued on my way.

I was becoming annoyed and depressed over this whole situation. The tunnel twisted this way and that, sharp at some point, which gave me the feeling I was doubling back, and then straightening out only to curve subtly one way and then the other. At one time, I thought I knew pretty much where I was under the farm, but now I was twisted around so that I had no idea; I could be under someone else's farm for all I knew. How could I have been so stupid to let myself be tricked into entering the basement? Well, since giant spiders were chasing me at the time, I didn't think about a sinkhole opening up in the basement floor. Now, here I was, hurt, dirty, tired and very late for work, with no idea if I was ever going to get up to the surface.

My train of thought was interrupted by the sound of cars and a fire siren. "Becky," I whispered, hope springing up inside me. I listened closely as the sound of the siren got closer and louder, and then screamed past toward my right, most likely continuing down the main road.

"I'm right next to the highway."

Hurrying as fast I as I could, I followed the sound as the tunnel turned sharply to the right and then off to the left. I then came upon a huge mass of tree roots; the stream continued flowing through the roots and down to what sounded like a steep drop and then onward toward, what I imagined, was under the highway and toward the tennis club.

The tree roots were huge, and with what I could make out in the dim light, the trunk of the tree wasn't sitting upright because it leaned precariously to one side. The tree was most likely dead, uprooted slightly from storms, wind and lots of water; the rest of the trunk was probably broken in half and lying on the ground above.

"I know where I am!"

Thanks to this mass of roots, I finally figured out how far away from the house I had gone. The tree was one of several old trees that had died and fell over at the edge of the pasture, near the main highway. John Jr. and I used to love to climb on them and play our pretend games when we were kids. Just the thought that I recognized where I was gave me a swell of relief and I smiled and shook my head at being so upset and worried earlier. The fire sirens screamed farther away, and then seemed to turn around and come back.

"I knew it, Becky's here and she's called the fire department to find me. She's figured it out!"

I was very excited over the idea of being rescued, but afraid as another thought entered my mind. *She doesn't know that I'm way out here.*

True enough, the pile of dead trees were a pretty good distance from the house, and no amount of shouting would be heard this far away.

How could I draw attention to myself way out here? I had to climb out from under the trees, but how? The ground around them was tightly packed, as I found out after trying to claw with my hands and drive my stick into the earth.

There had to be a way. I paced around the mangled old tree roots and almost decided to climb through them and push my way through the tree trunk, but the mounds of bugs and spiders entwined in the roots made me decided against it.

"Noooo waaay out Meeelisssaaa." William's voice echoed off the walls of the tunnel I had just come down, and it made the hair on my arms rise up.

"Oh, no," I moaned.

If he's talking again, it means he's watching me again, and if he's doing that, then he must be regaining strength. William getting strong again wasn't a good thing and I wasn't in the mood for more attacks from him.

I ferreted around the tree roots frantically, hopping on one foot over to where the water disappeared below the roots, and dodging the bugs and spiders, to around the other side where the trunk rose up out of the ground. I patted the earth around the trunk again, hoping to loosen some dirt and dig an opening, but there was no way. In the dark, I looked for something to push on, pull on, anything at all, and when all my efforts failed, I let out a deep disgusted sigh, and leaned onto the dark earth wall—and fell to the floor.

Picking myself up from the moist dirt and getting back into a standing position was more difficult than usual, based on the fact that I couldn't see the wall to place my hands on. The light streaming in through holes in the top of the tunnel was too far away to reach around the tree roots, which made this part of the tunnel extremely dark. Feeling from the floor to the wall was the only way I could find where to place my hands and stand on my good foot. Using this technique after I've found that wall, I was able to understand that the tunnel curved sharply to the right, and seemed to be doubling back on itself.

I peered into the pitch-blackness, squinting my eyes, and hoping that some small ray of sunlight would find a way to pierce the earth and show me the way. Unfortunately, that wasn't the case, and I was left with uneasiness in the pit of my stomach. Going into the darkness wasn't my idea of fun, but I had no other choice. It was either stay here and wait for William to come after me again, or feel my way down the black tunnel in hopes of making my way closer toward the house. Once I found my way, I would shout for Becky and the rescuers to pull me up out of the ground.

I released a deep breath, wiped my dirty hand on my pants, and started down the dark path.

Chapter Fourteen
The Rise of the Crystal

This new tunnel was cold and damp, causing me to shiver as I plodded along, patting the wall to make sure I was going in the right direction. I was very uncertain about advancing, fearful of falling into a deep hole. Traveling was even slower than usual as I used the walking stick to feel in front of me, before I hopped forward. The darkness was so dense I couldn't even see my hand in front of my face, and I started worrying if coming this way was a good idea.

I had no choice but to come this way, I thought, *there was no other way to go, and I might wind up closer to the house so I can yell and be rescued.* No matter how I justified the reason for following this dark tunnel, something kept nagging at the back of my mind.

It wasn't a good idea to leave myself so open and vulnerable like this; this time I wouldn't even see his attacks coming.

In my mind, I relived the scene of being trapped in that tight tunnel; sliding and pulling myself along on my knees and forearms, not being able to stand or turn around, while William's disgusting hand kept popping up from the dirt to gouge me and leave all kinds of bloody punctures on my body. Even though it all happened about an hour ago, it felt like it might have been days; being in the dark underground has a way of distorting time. I shivered at the memories, and then stopped dead in my tracks.

A string of quiet whispers floated up from behind me, like the gentle sound of a choir of female voices murmuring at once, saying nothing, yet speaking nonstop. Why I turned to look over my shoulder I'll never know, instinct I guess, it was so dark that I couldn't see if anything was there, yet the whispering sound was building, getting louder with each passing second. My heart hammered in my chest at the thought of William's approach.

Picking up the pace, I continued to slide my right hand along the wall and move as fast as I could. Swinging the walking stick with quick sweeps in front of my feet and taking longer strides, I wanted to get to the end of this tunnel in the worst way. The whispering was so loud I had the urge to scream at it to make it stop. I tried to ignore it, fear overtaking me as I hopped along, my breath coming in short gasps, sweet running down my face, my foot throbbing with pain, and my arms aching from all the upper body work I had to do. I couldn't tell which way I was going; I only knew I was still moving forward down the tunnel. At times the tunnel felt as if I was going around gentle arcs to the right or left, but I wasn't sure. I only knew I was still going the right way when the tunnel took a sharp left and I had to shade my eyes from the sunlight stabbing through another opening in the ground from above, which raised my spirits and chased the whispers away. There were obviously more starter sinkholes than could be seen on the surface, and I was grateful. Thanks to these many small sinkholes poking the tunnel ceiling every now and then, I could see where I was going and what was happening around me from time to time.

Sunlight shined through one of the fairly large openings, casting a wide ray of light across the entire width of the tunnel. I smiled, released a nervous sigh, and then rushed toward it; hope welling up inside me that I might be heard if I called out for help. I stopped directly in the path of the ray, and squinted, trying to look up through the hole. My eyes had become so used to the darkness that it hurt to look into the light but after a moment or two they adjusted, and I could see exactly where I was.

Through the baseball sized opening, I recognized the side of the barn and part of the stone wall from the paddock. I could also hear Becky shouting my name and the sound of a fire truck monitor.

"Becky! Becky, I'm out here, out here!"

I waited a bit, hoping she heard me, but with the fire trucks running, and the monitor making loud beeps and clicks every few seconds, I doubted they could.

I stood there for a minute, thinking and basking in the warmth of the sun when something sticking out of the side of the tunnel directly in front of me caught my eye. Curious, I gently touched it; it was hard and pointy, and the surface was like that of a crystal. Picking at the moist, lose dirt around it was enough for the object to reveal itself, and I gasped at the sight of the crystal pyramid, the same one I trapped William in eight years ago.

"Now I know exactly where I am," I said. "This is the same spot where Becky and I buried the crystal once I had William trapped inside."

I brushed mud off the sides and rubbed it on my already grimy pants to polish the pyramid a little. Closer examination revealed a crack close to the upper point, and I assumed that was how William got out. *Perhaps the damage happened when I dropped it in the hole we dug, or maybe from all the sinkhole activity.* The ground had been extremely active in this pasture over the years, secretly weaving sinkholes throughout the area.

"Didn't I have this in a little black bag?"

More routing around in the spot where I found the crystal pyramid exposed the rotted remains of what used to be the bag.

My musings were interrupted by a shuffling sound on the other side of the beam of light, making me look up quickly, and I froze once I noticed the slow moving form of William.

"That was my coffin," he gurgled still advancing and pointing at the crystal.

"And if it wasn't for this sinkhole, light wouldn't have shined on it, and you wouldn't have gotten out," I said fearfully, yet standing my ground.

William paused and spread his rotted bony arms wide, "This will be *your* coffin."

He sneered and took one giant step towards me, arms coiled for a quick strike. Even though he no longer actually had eyes, the sockets actually gave the impression of squinting angrily at me.

Alarmed, I thrust the crystal pyramid out in front of me as if it was a cross and William was the Devil. This act didn't sit well with him, and he snarled and rushed at me, clearing the short distance between us in a matter of seconds, but enough time for me to at least take a step back, putting the beam of light directly between us.

He slid to a halt and glared at me from across the barrier of sunlight. Trying to get through it would prove fatal to him, as I saw in the other tunnel, but he had an expression on his partially skeletal face that made me believe he was actually going to take a chance of getting hurt, just to get at me.

Stepping with his right foot, he placed almost the entire leg in the path of light, and then leaned forward to swipe at me. Instantly I staggered backward, keeping an arms-length between us. His actions only lasted a brief moment, for once smoke started rising up from his leg and foot he quickly withdrew.

"You will never leave here!"

"We'll see," I said in an angry tone. I was scared, but sick of being harassed by him, and no matter what, I wasn't going to just give up and let him do what he wanted.

Still holding the crystal out in front of me, I leaned forward into the sunlight, wiggling it at him and hoping to chase him away. Of course, there was always a chance he might figure out the crystal didn't have any more power and come after me anyway, but that was a chance I was willing to take. As I leaned forward, William took a small step back, and the action sent a thrill of excitement up my spine; *he* was scared of *me* for a change. This was so excellent; I had an ace up my sleeve and playing it for all it was worth.

"Ha!" I taunted, thrusting the crystal at him, then waving it all around in the beam of sunlight, which was something I shouldn't have done. William suddenly cocked his head to the side, gave me a questioning look, and then became angry. My little charade was over, and now it was my turn to retreat.

William hissed a low, sinister sound from deep in his throat and took a step closer to the light.

"Back off, William. I know how to use this."

"No you don't, and you will die for your foolishness," he said, raising a hand, gently placing it in the sunbeam, and gritting his exposed teeth as it began to smoke.

I kept the crystal out in front of me, even though I could see that the sun was beginning to go down and the sunbeam of light was losing its width. On the verge of panic once more, I held my ground for a short while longer until I felt a slight shudder in the palm of my hand. The crystal moved! I drew back my fingers a bit, trying to expose it to the light as much as possible, and it shuddered again. I think William noticed it too, because he paused and looked at it. At that moment, the crystal pyramid suddenly went wild; spinning out of my hand and hovering in the air, bands of light shot in all directions, illuminating the tunnel brighter than a flashlight, and I was able to catch a glimpse of the path beyond William.

The sudden awakening of the crystal totally freaked him out and he hissed some more, retreating while spinning, then disappeared into the earth tunnel wall.

I was relieved he was gone for the moment, but didn't think it would be for too much longer. The sun was going down and with a slight movement of the sunlight once more, the crystal stopped its colorful display and dropped lifeless to the ground. I picked it up and put it in my pocket; I may need it again. But for right now, I had to continue down the tunnel and get someone's attention before it became completely dark.

Chapter Fifteen
A Worthwhile Demise

Maneuvering down the dark tunnel wasn't as bad as it had been, especially since the crystal lit the way earlier and gave me an idea of which way to go. Time was ticking away. Soon the sun would go down, and then I would be at the mercy of William once more in his realm of darkness and without the help of the sun in any kind of way. With this in mind, I moved as quickly as I could; my arm sore from the stick and my foot throbbing with pain, I was dirty, uncomfortable, and desperately wanted to get out from under ground.

As I continued feeling my way along, I suddenly realized that I was touching not just dirt anymore, but stone and concrete.

"A foundation," I said in a hopeful tone. A foundation only meant one thing—the base of a building. But which one? There were so many in the area I was in: was it the barn, pigpen, or the stables. Any one of would mean I was still heading back toward the house, and that was a good thing.

Getting excited over the prospect of being rescued, I rushed along, flailing my hand in front of me in hopes of touching a door, or something that may lead into the barn. Why a door to the barn would be so far under ground, I didn't know, and I knew it was a stupid idea, but you never know. Back in the early eighteen hundreds buildings were built with strange passageways that only the original builders knew the purpose. Anything that would lead me out of this darkness would be welcome, and that idea urged me on.

However, there didn't seem to be an end to the foundation; it was wet, which was weird, and just kept going on and on.

"This *must* be to the barn," I said, deciding that no other structure would be this big. But I was also getting worried about the wetness of the wall, which meant the dirt floor was now mushy. My walking stick started to get stuck and I slipped numerous times, straining my back and left foot in the process. Where was the water coming from? The barn was no longer in use, so there was no need to have the troughs filled, unless there was a busted pipe and water was collecting in the base of the barn, and slowly trickling down through the foundation. Anything was possible; I just wanted to get out of this mud trap.

To make matters worse, the ceiling was beginning to get lower— again, and I instantly started worrying about being stuck in another tight tunnel. Even though the idea terrified me to death, I kept pressing on, concentrating so hard on feeling my way along the passage that I didn't hear the wet, sloppy footsteps coming up from behind me—until it was too late.

I was grabbed from behind with such force that I was lifted from my feet and tossed backwards. I landed on my back with a hard thump, still gripping my walking stick for dear life.

"I've had enough of this," William said in a low growl. "Your demise shall come now, before you have any more luck."

This was not a fair fight; I couldn't even see him in the dense blackness to defend myself, or even prepare for a thrashing. My only option was to kick out with my left foot and swing my stick like a madman.

Latching onto the middle of my walking stick, I swung it from side to side in a rowing fashion, and even though I wasn't making contact with him, I knew I was close due to his grunts and growls, most likely from dodging my swings. I kicked out with my left foot and struck something solid, and assumed it was William's leg because I suddenly felt him hit the dirt in front of me. Hoping that I had knocked his leg out from under him, I kicked out again, several times in a row, and my foot smacked him in the face. He snarled and grabbed my stick, but I wasn't about to let go and, because of that, felt myself lifted off the ground once more, and thrown forward.

I landed on my face this time, the impact nearly knocking the wind out of me, but I hung in there, groaning over the pain I felt, crawling forward along the ground, trying to get away and put some distance between my attacker and myself. However, William was coming up on me fast, his bony fingers grabbing at my feet and ankles, heavy footsteps landing with a slosh on either side of my legs, and his rancid stench wafting above me as he leaned over me.

I screamed when I felt him grab at my hair and finally found the strength to scramble to my feet, knocking him backwards in the process, and then ran blindly down the dark tunnel. Putting weight on my strained ankle wasn't a good thing but I had no choice. I forgot the pain shooting up my leg as I surged ahead, slamming into a bend in the low tunnel and turning the corner to the left.

Sunlight spilled through many baseball-sized hole in the ceiling, and it gave me a small advantage; at least I could see. Hearing him approach, I whirled around, now standing on my left foot again and readying my stick for an attack. He gained distance with each long, determined stride, not bothering to dodge the sunrays, nor letting them slow him down in the least. His sights were set on me and it didn't look like I was going to be able to run any further. This was it, the final showdown.

My heart pounded, my breath came in nervous gasps, and my whole body trembled with fear as I waited for him to close in on me.

"Die, Keeper of the Crystal," William taunted, rushing in close and reaching for my throat.

I jabbed the stick in his face, but he just shook it off after a brief pause. I jabbed him repeatedly, each time sticking it in a different part of his face, chest and shoulders. Nothing I did stopped him, and I silently blamed it on the ceiling being too low to swing the stick around. The more I raised it, the more it hit the ceiling, sending down a shower of dirt. That's all I needed, to have the whole ceiling cave in on me, then William would have his wish of the tunnel being my tomb.

I did a pretty good job jabbing with my stick while staggering around on my left foot and favoring my right ankle, for a little bit, but William soon found a way in through my defenses. He lashed out and struck me across the face with the back of his bony hand; the splintered bones making a gash across my left cheek. Staggering back into more light, I cried out in pain and touched the spot that now lay open.

William laughed and grabbed me by the arm, pulling me closer. I struck out with the stick, trying to ram it through his chest, but again the ceiling got in the way. More dirt rained down, getting in my mouth and eyes, and putting me at more of a disadvantage. This only amused my attacker, and he put his face close to mine, growled, and flung me backwards.

This time I only staggered against the wall, trying to catch myself and keep hold of the stick. It was then I heard a horrible crack and my ankle gave out from under me. The pain was too much to bear and I screamed as tears rolled down my cheeks. I couldn't do this anymore. How was I supposed to fight this creature, this thing that wouldn't die and that was so much stronger than I was? Well, one thing was sure, I was going down fighting, no matter what.

Planting my left foot firmly, and resting slightly on my broken ankle, I spun the stick once again in a rowing fashion, but this time like a crazed rower. It kept hitting the ceiling, dirt pouring down in clumps, but I didn't care, this was my last stand.

William stepped in close and backhanded the stick from my grasp. It twirled madly, end over end, and stuck like a javelin in the ceiling, just before his cold, bony hands clasped around my neck. He shook me like a rag doll and tightened his grip, but I stared into his lifeless eye sockets as I tried to pry his hands off me.

Dirt poured endless down from the spot where the stick had stuck, building up around my feet and slowly inching up to my claves. This was it for me, the end, William's grip was too strong. I couldn't use my left foot to kick with because my right was now completely useless, and no matter what I did with my hands I couldn't make him let go. The dirt was going to pour down, burying me while the undead continued to squeeze the life out of me, and I could do nothing.

Any sunlight I could see from the holes in the tunnel's ceiling started to go dark, the image of William's mangled face began to get blurry. I couldn't breathe, or swallow; feeling the bones in my neck begin to contract under the force of his grip.

Isn't there any hope for me?

At that moment, the ceiling gave way, falling completely in to expose a huge hole. William let go of me, screaming and shading his face from the sunlight that poured in, engulfing him in an immense beam of light. I staggered back, instantly gasping for air, and rubbing my neck.

Looking up, I could see the sky, the trees, and the buildings around me. I was even closer to the house than before! However, my happy thoughts were suddenly interrupted by William's screams of agony. He was on his knees in the pile of dirt, shivering and grasping at all the places on his body that were smoking. I slid along the wall, putting space between us. I wasn't sure what was going to happen, and didn't want to be too close.

While continuing to tremble, he raised his left hand up and looked at it; smoke now seeping out of every place on his arm, then he turned his head and snarled at me.

"I should have won; victory was mine!"

I didn't know what to say; I just stared at him and kept my distance.

His arm suddenly burst into flames and he threw his head back and let out a blood-curdling scream. I watched in horror as his other arm caught fire, and then became a chain reaction with every part of him spontaneously igniting until his whole body was an inferno.

Still on his knees, William trashed around, swinging his arms wildly in an effort to put out the flames, but nothing worked. His crazed efforts and high-pitched wails soon died away as he became nothing more than a pile of ash, blending in with the dirt where he kneeled. I stood still, breathing hard and staring at the spot where he had been, waiting for him to spring up out of the earth and come after me again, but nothing happened. Inching forward, I bent down and nudged the ash and dirt with my hand then jerked it back quickly, afraid that William's hand might shoot up from the dirt and grab me, but that didn't happen either.

"Is it over?" I looked around the tunnel and then up through the hole. "I'm free, I can get out of here now."

Chapter Sixteen
An Uncertain Rescue

The hole was wide, but not very deep, and with a little effort I was able to stick my head and arms up above the surface.

"Hey!" I waved and shouted to anyone that might be able to hear me. "Hey, over here!"

It was now becoming dusk, and the gloom made it hard to see my surroundings, yet I could hear dogs barking and assumed it was rescuer workers still looking for me. They haven't given up and that was something in my favor.

"Hey, help! Help, over here!" I shouted again while waving my arms frantically. "Becky, down here!" I was beginning to get upset that no one heard me and started to worry if anyone would ever find me. However, my fears were laid to rest when a dog sounded off and the pounding of many paws closed in. "Help!" I called repeatedly until two large German Shepards ran over to me with their handlers close behind.

"Are you Melissa?" one of the handlers asked.

"Yes," I said breathlessly, reaching for the men eagerly. "Please get me out of here."

"Are you hurt?" the other man asked.

"I think my ankle is broken."

The second man quickly radioed for help; requesting rope, stretcher, and medical supplies. I was anxious for them to lift me up, however I was still down rather deep and they might be afraid of hurting me more. I knew the worst was over, but became a little nervous when the dogs circled the edges of the hole, sniffing, and whining with worry. They knew something in this hole wasn't right, animals can always tell, and it made my anxiety build.

"Can you *please* just get me up?"

"One moment miss, they're coming," the first man said, motioning with his hand that I should be still a moment longer.

The sound of an engine told me the paramedics were driving their truck along the old tractor path that ran around the backside of the house, to meet us in front of the barn. They backed the truck up very close, and then a few more men jumped out with medical cases in their hands.

I wish they wouldn't take so long or be so cautious, I just wanted to get out of this hole and away from William's ashes.

Two men jumped into the hole with me, stepping on the ashes and stirring them up, which seemed to upset the dogs even more as they backed away, barking and whining. Yet no one paid any attention to them; the men just lowered a stretcher down into the opening, gently picked me up, laid me down, and strapped me to it tight. Immediately panic overtook me. Here I was, still in the hole, strapped down with no way to move, and these men weren't even talking to me. For all I knew, they were under some sort of spell put on them by William. I didn't care that he wasn't here in a physical form, the reactions of the dogs put me on guard.

"Hey, hey what are you guys doing? Get me out of this hole, please. Ouch, not so tight!" They didn't respond to anything I said, and I looked fearfully at each of their faces, searching for some sign that maybe they weren't under a spell and I was just being paranoid.

Their expressions were calm and their skin pale, but no strange look in their eyes or faces to indicate an evil presence existed, however it wasn't enough to make me feel any better.

"Becky! Where's my sister? Becky, where are you?"

"Melissa!"

Just the sound of her voice sent a wave of relief washing over me, and I looked up through the opening to see her drop on her knees near the edge and smile down at me.

"What took you so long?"

"Oh, shut up, I was so worried about you," she said, eyes welling up with tears. "Come on guys, get her up."

Welcome words she spoke just then, and the men complied by standing the stretcher straight up, and very gently lifting me out of the hole. I was so happy to be out of that dirt coffin, but couldn't help to repeatedly look over my shoulder at the now scattered pile of ashes. Nothing was happening, there were no more spells on people, no more mind games and illusions produced by William; I was free from his torment and would soon be going home.

"What exactly happened to you?" Becky said, climbing into the back of the truck with the paramedics and holding my hand as they stuck an IV in it.

I told her my story from the point when my cell phone died and how I started to walk to the neighbor's house, how spiders chased me to the sinkhole in the basement, and all I had encountered with William deep underground.

"Most of the illusions were so real, but never actually happened, and those I thought were illusions *did* actually happened," I said, showing her the gouges in my leg and side left by William's claw-like hands.

"Where is William now?" Becky whispered.

"Down there," I indicated with my eyes toward the hole. "That hole opened up and the last bit of sunlight hit him full force, making him go up in flames. His ashes are down there. One of the guys stepped in them like it was no big deal."

"Most likely because he doesn't know, and was only concerned about getting you out of there," Becky said, wiping dirt from my face.

"Becky, this whole place is full of sinkholes, they run under the entire farm. I really think we all need to get going before something else happens."

"Okay, I'll go tell Dennis to drive your car and follow us to the hospital," Becky said, getting up.

"Dennis? Who's Dennis?"

"Ahhh, my new…friend," Becky said in a hesitating manner.

Just then a fresh-faced young man with dark hair appeared at the back doors of the rescue truck and Becky smiled, first at him, and then at me.

"Dennis, this is my stepsister Melissa."

I nodded at him, and then smiled at her; silently hoping this meant she finally found someone to share her life with, but knowing it also meant we wouldn't be spending as much time together.

Moments later, we were finally driven around to the front of the house and parked in the gravel driveway, while Dennis got in my car and started it right up. I shook my head and couldn't help feeling that I was such a fool to think my car wouldn't start earlier in the day. It was all just a trick to get me out of the car, which had been the first big mistake, and as I thought of all I did wrong today, something kept nagging at the back of my mind and waves of worry surged through me.

"We really should be going," I said to Becky and the paramedics. "We need to get away from this house."

"I know you had a trying day, Melissa, but it's just a house and William is finally gone forever," Becky said, practically laughing at me.

"It's not that, it's…something…else."

Just at that instant the ground began to quake and vibrate, rattling the truck windows and making the dogs howl.

"Get us out of here!" I said to the driver, twisting around on the stretcher and looking out of the open truck doors.

All the commotion was coming from the house, it shook and rocked like something was pushing up from underneath; the windows shattered and walls began to crumble, and through the thickness of the dusk I was able to see the ground surrounding the house begin to give way.

Chapter Seventeen
The Fate of the Old House

The ground from the outskirts of the house broke away and crumbled inward, weakening the foundation of the old house and forcing it to slide from side to side. The trembling became more intense, and it felt like it was radiating from underneath, possibly from the very center. Right away I thought of William and wondered if perhaps his ashes had become whole and he was trying to rise up once more. Fear mounted deep inside and I reached for Becky, grabbing her arm and tugging her close.

"Get everyone to back away!"

"Duh, we're doing that!"

Rescue trucks, fire trucks, and the few cars parked around the driveway were backed out to Wakefield Road, and then there was nothing more to do but watch.

The old farmhouse continued to rock and lean from side to side, steadily crumbling as the foundation heaved under what felt like a tremendous force. Men shouted warnings, the dogs barked and howled, and Becky and I clung to each other in desperation. The rumbling surrounded us and it felt as if we all would be subjected to the same fate as the old house. But that was all about to change, for in a blink of an eye the house gave a final shudder then dropped out of sight, leaving nothing but a huge cloud of dust.

The trembling from the ground stopped, only to be replaced by a dying echo from the house falling apart—somewhere. It was now totally dark and no one could see exactly what just happened.

"Bring the truck," someone called, and the fire truck, with the tall ladder, backed up as close as it dared to the edge of the black pit. A large, bright spotlight was shined into the darkness to see what happened to the old farmhouse.

"It fell into a sinkhole," one of the paramedics said, looking out the back of the truck.

"Sinkhole?" I said, favoring my ankle and turning around to look out of the open truck doors even more.

Sure enough, the old house had been sucked down into a very large, very deep sinkhole, and took with it the old hand pump, half the huge maple tree, and a few of the small buildings close to the back of the house.

"So, that's it then," I said more to myself than to Becky.

"It's finally and completely over now Melissa. William is gone and has no place left to haunt; not the house, not the ground under it," Becky said, patting my arm.

"Let's hope."

"He's not coming back. You did it, whatever it was exactly, and his spell is broken," Becky said.

"I hope you're right. It's been eight years since the last time we thought we got rid of him and he managed to get out of this," I produced the cracked crystal and Becky's face took on a sober look.

"You found it?"

"Close to where you pulled me out of that hole back there," I indicated with a nod back toward the barn.

"I'm certain this time that we're rid of him forever. Now, let's get you out of here." Becky gave me a quick kiss on the forehead and jumped out of the back of the rescue truck.

I tried to watch as she got into her car and Dennis got into mine, until the doors securely closed and we pulled away from the wreckage.

It was hard to believe that my torment from William was finally over; no more hauntings, no more pain, no more tricks and illusions and, hopefully, most of all, no more bad dreams. I released a deep sigh and settled back onto my cot. Perhaps now, for the first time in eight years, I could actually put my past behind me and concentrate on my future. And perhaps now, starting tomorrow, I can produce the type of design for the front of Goulies Cereal that Mr. McDermond had in mind and not cringe at what "scary" *really* is.

Printed in the United States
25232LVS00005B/67-114